UNICOR...
COLORING BOOK

YOU'RE NEVER TOO OLD TO COLOR!

To:

From:

YOU'RE NEVER TOO OLD TO COLOR!

ISBN: 9798326372147

UNICORN
COLORING BOOK

YOU'RE NEVER TOO OLD TO COLOR!

SCAN HERE

FOLLOW SALLE COLORS ON SOCIAL
MEDIA FOR GIVEAWAYS!

Frost

Bliss

Sunburst

Blossom

Fleur

Fable

Glory

Dewdrop

Mystic

Moonshadow

Wysteria

Sprinkle

Sparkles

Whimsy

Amara

Solice

Opal

Rosebud

Flair

Stardust

Shimmer Flame

Luminescence

Moonbeam

Dreamcatcher

Flowerbell

Glimmer

Aurora

Mirage

Breeze

Melody

Meadow

Ember

Nova

Starlight

Azure

Dreamer

Glade

Rainbow Dash

Twinkle

Moonstone

Haze

Harmony

Fancy

Marigold

Dazzle

Silver Wing

Shimmer Flame

Sky Dancer

Luminara

Whisper

UNICORN COLORING BOOK

YOU'RE NEVER TOO OLD TO COLOR!

Thank you!

Your purchases help Salle Colors
create more coloring books!

Salle Colors

YOU'RE NEVER TOO OLD TO COLOR!

Made in United States
Troutdale, OR
07/03/2024